W9-AWV-336

ALMOST TIME

Gary D. Schmidt & Elizabeth Stickney
Illustrated by G. Brian Karas

CLARION BOOKS | Houghton Mifflin Harcourt | Boston   New York

For Carolyn and Samantha
—A.E.S. and G.D.S.

For Greg—brother, friend,
and master maple syrup maker
—G.B.K.

When Ethan had to eat his pancakes with applesauce instead of maple syrup one Sunday morning, he knew it was almost sugaring time.

"Is the sap running yet?" he asked.
Dad shook his head. "Not until the days get warmer."

That afternoon, Ethan took his sled to the Big Hill.
It was a sunny day, so he left his hat and his scarf and
his mittens at home.

But the day wasn't warm.

Next Sunday morning, Ethan's dad made a pan
of corn bread. No syrup.

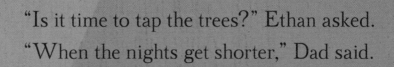

"Is it time to tap the trees?" Ethan asked.
"When the nights get shorter," Dad said.

At bedtime that night, Ethan thought there might be
some daylight still coming through the window.

But there wasn't enough to find Roosevelt.

Next Sunday morning, Ethan stirred raisins and walnuts
into his bowl of oatmeal. No syrup.

When he bit down on a walnut, he discovered something.
"My tooth is loose!" he said.

His father inspected. "I expect it will fall out before long."
"How long?" asked Ethan.
"About as long as it takes the sap to start running," Dad said.

Now Ethan had two things to wait for.

But the days were still cold.

And the nights were still long.

And his tooth would not come out.

The next Sunday morning,
Ethan's dad made eggs and toast.

Ethan tried not to think about
maple syrup in the afternoons
when he slid down the Big Hill,

or when he turned on his lamp
at night,

or when he wiggled his very,
very loose tooth during school,

until . . .

His dad was waiting when he got off the bus.

"How's that tooth?" he asked. Ethan smiled, to show him.

"So is the sap going to run now?" asked Ethan.

His dad smiled, to show him.

Every afternoon that week, and all day Saturday, Ethan and Dad
hauled buckets of sap from the trees

and tended the fire beneath the pans . . .

. . . as the sap boiled and boiled.

And early on Sunday morning, when there was already a little light in the sky, Ethan poured sweet maple syrup on his pancakes.

E
473-5299

Clarion Books • 3 Park Avenue, New York, New York 10016

Text copyright © 2020 by Gary D. Schmidt and Elizabeth Stickney • Illustrations copyright © 2020 by G. Brian Karas

All rights reserved. For information about permission to reproduce selections from this book, write to trade.permissions@hmhco.com or to

Permissions, Houghton Mifflin Harcourt Publishing Company, 3 Park Avenue, 19th Floor, New York, New York 10016.

Clarion Books is an imprint of Houghton Mifflin Harcourt Publishing Company. • hmhbooks.com

The illustrations in this book were executed in pencil and digital color. • The text was set in Bazhanov. • Book design by Sharismar Rodriguez

Library of Congress Cataloging-in-Publication Data | Names: Schmidt, Gary D., author. | Stickney, Elizabeth, author. | Karas, G. Brian, illustrator.

Title: Almost time / Gary D. Schmidt and Elizabeth Stickney ; illustrated by G. Brian Karas. | Description: Boston ; New York : Clarion Books,

Houghton Mifflin Harcourt, [2019] | Summary: Ethan eagerly anticipates making maple syrup with his father, but it will not be time until the days are warmer,

the nights shorter, and Ethan's loose tooth falls out. | Identifiers: LCCN 2018051995 | ISBN 9780544785816 (hardcover picture book)

Subjects: CYAC: Expectation (Psychology)—Fiction. | Fathers and sons—Fiction. | Maple syrup—Fiction.

Classification: LCC PZ7.S3527 Alm 2019 | DDC [E]—dc23 | LC record available at https://lccn.loc.gov/2018051995

Manufactured in Malaysia • TWP 10 9 8 7 6 5 4 3 2 1

4500775951